Marching Bands Are Just Homeless Orchestras

Half-Empty Thoughts, Vol. 1

By Tim Siedell

Illustrated by Brian Andreas

StoryPeople Press

ISBN-13: 978-0-9745516-2-3
ISBN-10: 0-9745516-2-7

Copyright © 2010 by Tim Siedell
Illustrations Copyright © 2010 by Brian Andreas

This book is a work of fiction. Names, characters, places, and incidents either are products of the author's imagination or are used fictitiously. Any resemblance to actual events or locales or persons, living or dead, is entirely coincidental.

All rights reserved. No part of this book may be reproduced or transmitted in any form or by any means, electronic or mechanical, including photocopying, recording, or by any information storage and retrieval system, without permission in writing from the Publisher.

StoryPeople Press
P.O. Box 7
Decorah, IA 52101
USA
563.382.8060
563.382.0263 FAX
800.476.7178

storypeople@storypeople.com
www.storypeople.com
www.storypeoplepress.com

Library of Congress Control Number: 2010914112

First Edition: November, 2010

This book is made from 30% post-consumer paper and has been organically recycled using free range chickens over the course of eons. Enjoy!

Introduction

Ever feel like your lack of power and wealth might be holding you back? Of course you do.

The truth is you and I are a lot alike. You put your pants on one leg at a time, and I've watched people put their pants on one leg at a time. Like you, I enjoy the simple things in life because complex things, like math and mechanical pencils, are unnecessarily vexing. No doubt, you have aspirations in life. Me, too. And if yours involves digging up and reuniting the skeletons of the Rat Pack, we have more in common than I originally thought. That's good.

But we're different, too. I, for example, know the medical term for black lung disease. So there's that. Other dissimilarities probably include my home state (Nebraska), my choice for corrective vision (glasses), and my love of cute photos sent via email (low, borderline robot-level). I also own a cat. And if you own a cat, as well, I doubt it's named Olive. And if it is named Olive, I still doubt that we're talking about the same cat.

I'm confident there are enough similarities between us that you can flip through this book, nod your head in agreement a few times, and generally feel good about paying money for it or going to the hassle of stealing it from the store. And hopefully there are enough differences between us that you won't feel like you're reading something you could have written yourself. Because, let's face it, you're probably not a great writer. No offense. Statistically speaking.

I'd like to thank Brian Andreas for bringing his unique artistic style to this book. I've seen him draw in person. Let's just say he puts as much time into his trademark doodles as I put into the words. And let's just say we had plenty of time to do other things together, like walk down to a Mexican restaurant and order steak.

Special thanks as well to my supportive wife, my two daughters, and, for reasons that they will not understand unless they read this book, my neighbors. I would also like to thank the Internet, without which I would never have been able to diagnose myself as having every major disease.

Tim Siedell

Marching Bands Are Just Homeless Orchestras

Slightly comforted by the fact that in some parallel universe I'm insanely rich and successful. Slightly concerned I'm a country music star.

You can call it brunch if you like, but I'm still getting two more meals.

The fact the first step of a 12-step program isn't "join a 12-step program" makes me wonder what else they're leaving off the list.

I hopped out of bed this morning like Fred Astaire. Or anyone else, really, who has been dead for 20 years.

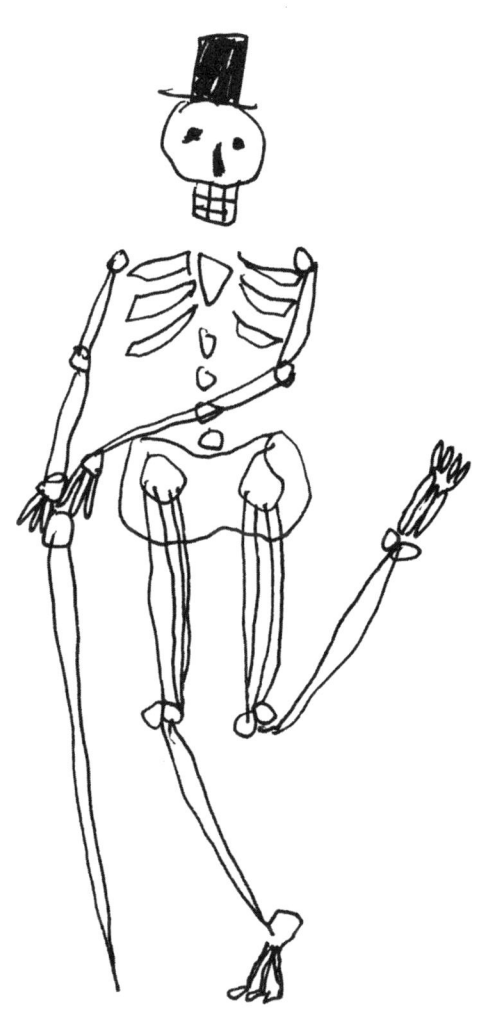

I think Johnny Cash wore black because it's slimming. It was either that or be known as the Man in Vertical Stripes.

Technology is all well and good until someone hits you in the head with a rock.

So organizing my desk is procrastination? Abe Lincoln would say I'm sharpening my axe. Plus, he'd love the tiny log house made of pencils.

I love my new winter beard so much it
would be the first thing I save
from a burning building.

I wouldn't want to spend eternity with 70 virgins. It's like being a middle school teacher without the summers off.

I wouldn't say I'm antisocial as much as I'd say it's hard to meet interesting people in an attic.

No fair. Black people get the entire month of February, while fat people only get a Tuesday.

I would like martini bars better if they didn't attract the kind of people who like martini bars.

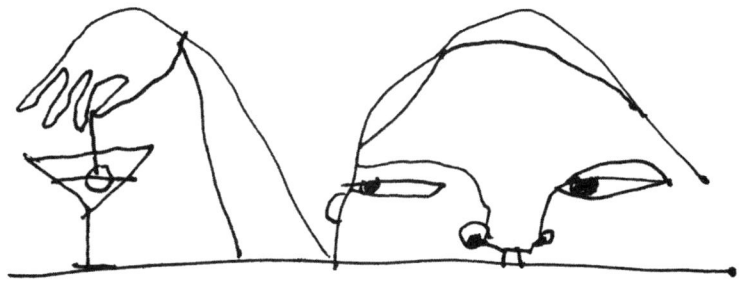

I don't like this recent trend of so many people being younger than me.

All we hear about is pain on Wall Street and Main Street. How about Sesame Street? People are living in trash cans there.

Half of the appeal of staying up late is the total absence of morning people.

On the bright side, I think my neighbor has almost completed his Giant Backyard Noise Machine.

I have long ago given up the dream of
rocking down to Electric Avenue,
let alone taking it higher.

A new study finds people with thin thighs
die sooner. But not as soon as people
who point this out to women
with big thighs.

To me, the glass is half full. Yes, of doom
and despair, but still.

Some men prefer Betty. Others, Wilma.
Then there are those of us who
keep eyeing all the huge
dinosaur steaks.

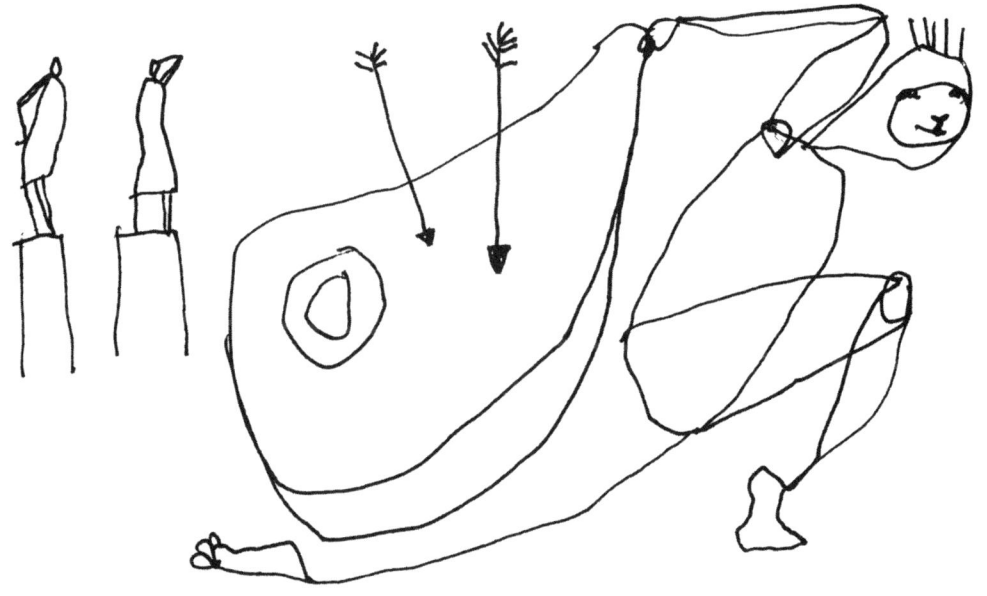

I like doing paperwork because it
brings me closer to nature.

The economy is so bad I just saw a guy in
the back of a limo hand another guy
in a limo a bottle of generic,
yellow mustard.

Edgar Bergen and Cormac McCarthy.
That would be some
dark, depressing
ventriloquism.

The Sunday afternoon nap is the
Champagne of Beers of Naps.

Work your way up to juggling chainsaws by starting with small chainsaws.

The restaurant across the street has gone out of business. I will miss wondering how it stays open.

Ugh, writer's block. My third most dreaded block behind artery block and block party.

Thankfully, my perimeter defenses worked.
The doorbell alerted me of human
presence, so I stayed away
from the door.

At my daughter's cross country meet.
Seeing girls run away from me
brings back a flood of middle
school memories.

If a mime performs in the forest, and
nobody is there to see him,
it's all for the best.

If I were a drug dealer, I'd brand mine "No"
and explain to kids that their parents
told them to ask for it by name.

Got my to-do list and bucket list mixed up.
I guess my household projects will just
have to wait until after I win a Tony.

I didn't realize my life was the director's cut.
I don't need all this extra crap.

The best time to start applying heat and
pressure to coal in order to make
diamonds is 300 million years
ago. The second best
time is now.

Life would be easier if I could just breathe
coffee. Except for the astronaut helmet
full of scalding hot liquid, I guess.

Split down gender lines. Final baby kitty name results: 3 votes for Olive, 1 for Murderface.

When you order your Thai food extra spicy you are, in essence, giving someone permission to murder you from the inside out.

I accidentally saw a little bit of daytime television. The eye wash station is already paying for itself.

People in movies always seem like they're having way too much fun when they're at the movies.

My bed is calling me. And trust me, no matter what the salesman says, that's an unnecessary and obnoxious bed feature.

Scientists are close to creating three-parent babies. This is exactly the kind of breakthrough that could
save the sitcom.

The problem with throwing a Hulk tantrum at work is the inevitable walk
to the parking garage
without a shirt.

Business idea: Richard Gere lookalikes wearing white, naval uniforms who pick you up and carry you wherever you want
to go.

Neighbor just asked me to watch for a
delivery while he's out of town.
This is the neighbor who can't
read body language.

On May 17, 1846, Antoine-Joseph Sax invented the '80s soundtrack.

Misery may love company, but be prepared to take your shoes off before going into the living room. And don't expect snacks.

Riverboat Demolition Derby. I can't be the first to suggest that.

I hope Lady Gaga donates her old costumes to homeless shelters. Because that would be hilarious.

My primary objective in any meeting is to end the meeting.

I'm hoping for a Paul Simon kind of day. Short and pleasant enough. None of that Garfunkel crap.

I overheard a co-worker talking about the tranny in his truck. I don't judge.

I'm sick of hearing about bad unemployment figures. These folks have enough concerns without worrying about body image.

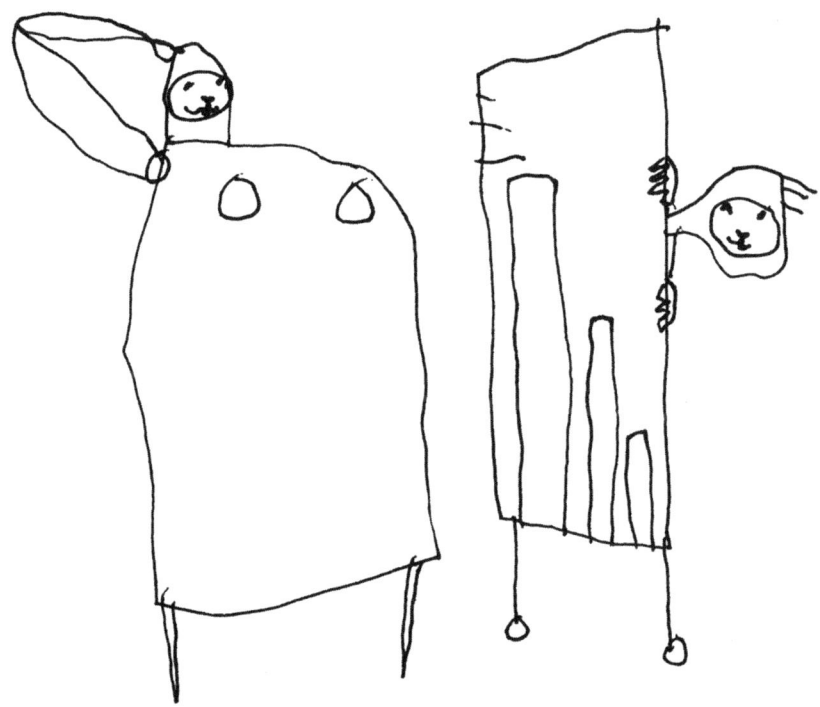

Heated flatbed scanners, people. I shouldn't have to freeze my rear end off every time I email my landlord.

The scariest movie monster has to be the Invisible Man. Because he's a naked man. And he might be sitting on your sofa.

I must have slept like a log last night, because I feel like someone chopped me up and stacked me neatly by the garage.

Avoided a copay by having my annual physical at Antiques Roadshow. Clean bill of health. Plus, I found out I'm worth $150.

I'm banned from driving muscle cars
because I just tested positive
for Yoplait lowfat yogurt.

I bet the town hall meetings in Germany
were full of protesters comparing
Hitler to Hitler.

It's my way or the highway. Unless your way
involves actual highways, in which case
this shouldn't be construed as an
expressed endorsement.

My weirdo neighbors never talk to me
unless they want something,
like for me to get out from
under their couch.

I didn't have to chew my leg off to get out of that boring meeting, but doing so certainly sent a strong message.

That Indian dinner was so authentic I think I hate Pakistan.

Screw the Mayan calendar. This Dilbert desk calendar speaks of nothing beyond December 31, 2010.

When is the best time to start training a kitten to hold a knife?

New cat games: mouse, mouse, knife
(rough concept - might need some work)

We need some new mythological creatures.
I propose: Scentofawomantaur. Half Al
Pacino, half horse. Speaks in hoo-ahs.
Nonsequitaur. Half man, half horse,
half-grilled cheese sandwich.

I want to live to see great-grandchildren.
But instead of taking care of myself,
I'll just push my kids to get
married at 9.

The monogrammed initials on your cuffs
have foiled my plans to kill you and
wear your shirt. Well played, sir.

Putting on weight for a film role in case I'm ever asked to play myself in a movie.

& still amazingly light on his feet

My wife and daughters are sick while I
feel fine. It occurs to me that flu
immunity might be tied to
sports trivia knowledge.

One thing this bad economy can't take
away from me is the simple joy
of eating raw diamonds.

I'm at that point on a huge writing project
where I ponder disguises and
fake passports.

Spent the entire evening wrestling with a new wireless printer. Probably should have spent that time trying to set it up.

Now might be a good time to put money in the stock market. I would, but I lost all my money in the stock market.

I don't crave being driven around in outlandishly long automobiles anymore. Thank you, limousine patch.

My oldest daughter is now a teenager. I've prepared for this day by preemptively hating myself for the last 40 years.

I'll keep wearing fur as long as young actresses are willing to punish me by posing naked.

To prevent cabin fever, I'm having my doctor inject me with a small amount of microscopic cabins.

My neighbors are stealing my Wi-Fi. I'm changing the password as soon as I get out from under their bed.

Congress is attacking the evil on Wall Street while completely ignoring the nightmare on Elm Street.

A conference call is like a bus ride. I want it to end as quickly as possible, preferably with nobody talking to me.

A bread bowl is just a poor man's meat bowl.

We hate what we do not understand. I'm not really sure what that phrase means, but it's a stupid whore.

Another day without anyone assassinating me. I'm practically the anti-McKinley.

Can't decide if my evening should be full of medication or heavy machinery.

Reggae music is awesome for five minutes.

A friend told me I'm out of touch. I laughed so hard I almost peed my Hammer pants.

Hey ladies, if you don't want me staring at your tattoos, maybe you should lock your front door before showering.

Morning people are the North Korea of my personal Axis of Evil. Crazy and loud, but ultimately unable to do any real damage to me.

Just finished up an interesting water cooler conversation. That guy sure knew a lot about water coolers.

The first rule of Scrapbooking Club is to tell everyone we're in a Fight Club.

I'm at a coffee-or-murder fork in the road. Either way, I doubt I'll be getting much sleep tonight.

Mamas, don't let your babies be cowboys, either. No baby cowboys. We thought that was obvious, but now lawyers are involved.

If I must forget things in my old age, let's start by forgetting the fact I used to remember everything.

My "Shakespeare in the Parking Garage" production was a failure. Seemed to be some confusion about whether or not we were actually performing on level 2B.

This week is so slow whoever plays it in a movie will win an Oscar.

One door closes, another opens. Unless they're Dutch doors. Then we're talking half-door increments and the math confuses me.

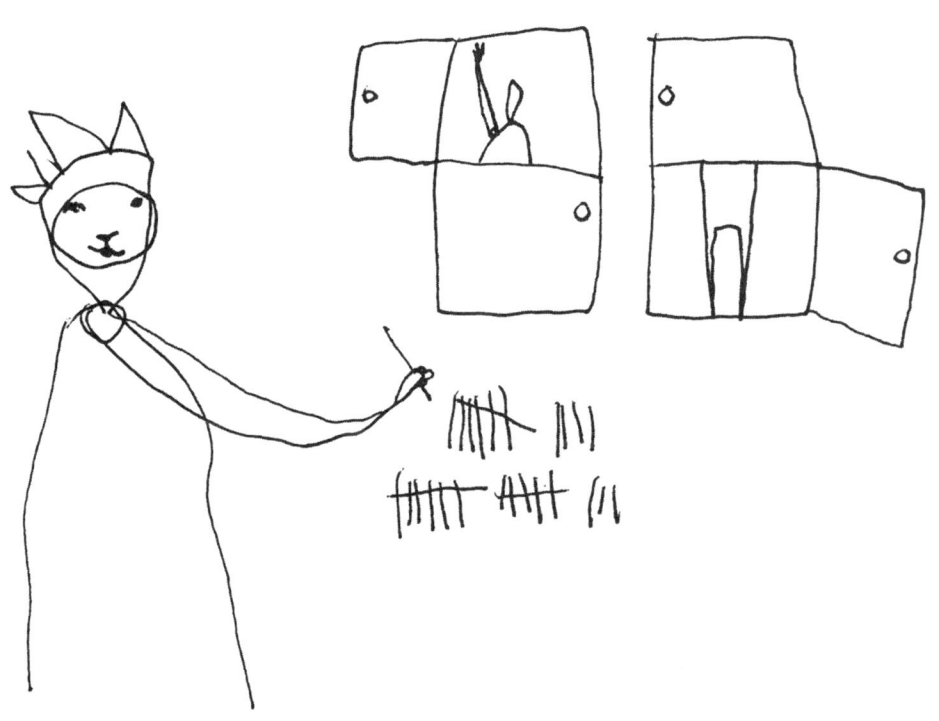

Don't be offended if I kick your butt
but don't take your name.
I'm horrible with names.

He's been marinating in honey for years.
Don't tell me a rack of Winnie-the-Pooh
ribs wouldn't be tasty.

I'm glad when a concert advertises limited
seating because parking is a real pain at
those unlimited seating venues.

A couple of afternoon martinis never killed anyone. Which is why I'm drinking a lot more than that.

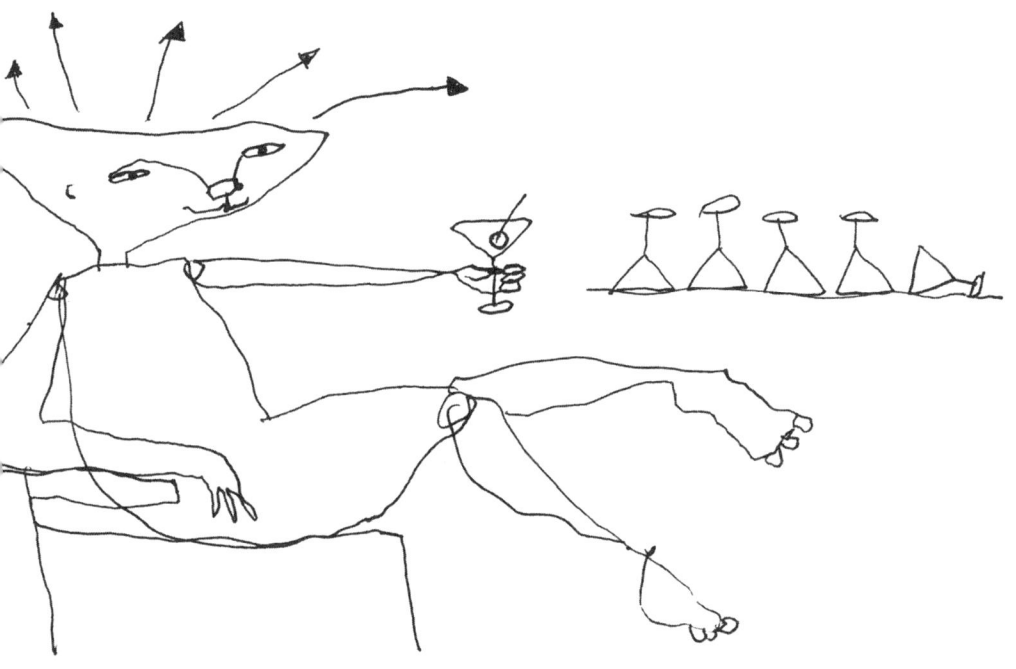

As a kid, I had lots of time but very few quarters. As an adult, I have many quarters and so little time. FORGIVE ME, CENTIPEDE!

———

A panic room seems overindulgent. I can panic in any room.

———

As adorable as my cat acts around laser pointers, I'm just not all that impressed with his PowerPoint presentations.

Edison said genius is 99 percent perspiration.
So, whatever you do, don't drink it.

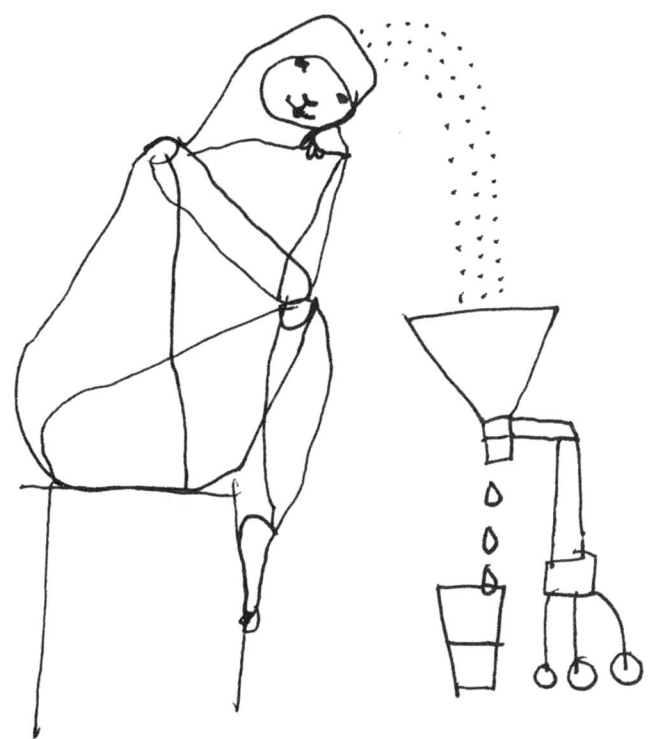

A midlife crisis is just teen angst
with disposable income.

When I want something a little healthier
than an ice cream sandwich, I usually
go for an ice cream salad.

Reinstalling Microsoft Office on a Friday night.
There are so many sad layers to this,
I feel like an Olive Garden lasagna.

I bet the hardest part of being a sushi chef
is cutting the heads off mermaids.

Never trust anyone under 30 lbs. Especially when it comes to driving directions. Babies are liars.

Night people could take over the world if we weren't so busy finding something good on TV.

By the third time he's sent out to pick up a pile of clothes in an alley, I bet Clark Kent's intern is totally weirded out.

I'm calling it a night because I'm too tired to get out a thesaurus.

Had a minor confrontation with a neighbor. Now my shoes are completely covered in neighbor.

Just invented Strip Miming. I charge $250 an hour to not do it. Franchises available.

November always reminds me of Homecoming dances in high school. I think it's the No part.

There's cautious optimism on Wall Street.
Now stock brokers are only jumping
out of first-floor windows.

Prepping for jury duty. I want to look smart every time I object to something.

If Clifford were a Big Red Cat, everyone would be dead.

Leprechauns are freaky, but Chakakhanchauns are horrifying. If you hear the opening of "I Feel For You" in the woods, run.

What is productivity, really? I will ponder this question while sitting in my new, manila folder igloo.

And would it kill today's rap artist to put on some colorful pants? Some of us really liked the colorful pants.

———

Keep slumping down in your chair. Slowly. Then, when nobody can see you, slide under table. Compose yourself. Roll out door. If you escape unnoticed, great. If the other meeting participants see you roll away, my experience is they won't stop you.

———

Saturday night just logged me out due to inactivity.

Don't drink and drive. Also, don't eat corn on the cob and drive.

For the record: a computer on its deathbed just wishes it could keep working. Family means nothing to these bastards.

Life will be less complicated once my cat learns how to tie his own bow ties.

You have to bust some moves to make a dance omelet.

Robert Frost was a genius. I just took the road less traveled and it ended up being a shortcut to Walmart®.

I had planned to teach my robot right and wrong, but so far I'm pretty impressed with its choice of victims.

Making travel plans for my birthday.
I think 1994 sounds nice.

Rude. My neighbor across the street keeps looking directly into my rifle scope.

If Death hands you lemons, just eat them.
Peels and all. It really doesn't matter
at that point.

Ate an Egg MacGuffin this morning, although it didn't really have anything to do with the rest of my breakfast.

As a general rule of thumb, I prefer one per hand. But I'll make some exceptions.

Giving this positive outlook thing the old college try. Which means I'll only try on Tuesdays and Thursdays.

Business Casual means your numbers don't have to add up, right?

All the world's a stage? Or the world is my oyster? I need to know so I can wear the right shoes.

I've been feeling better about myself ever since I started calling the fetal position the victory position.

Don't you hate it when time travelers from the future want a photo with you but then refuse to say why they're laughing?

If I were stuck on a deserted island with just one book, I'd want it to be so huge I could sail home on it.

About the Author

Tim Siedell currently meets all constitutional requirements to be the President of the United States. He is also an aspiring billionaire. He lives about as far away from New York and Los Angeles as you can get at the same time along with his wife, two daughters, some pets, and a crippling sense of self-loathing. You can find him on Twitter as @badbanana.

About the Artist

Brian Andreas is a California artist whose paintings, sculptures, and books have delighted people all over the world for more decades than he will admit. Still recovering from Midwestern winters, he currently lives in the Bay Area with canvas, wire, wooden boards, and other tools for storytelling never too far out of reach. His work is shown and collected internationally.

About StoryPeople

StoryPeople Press is located in the heart of America (That's right... Iowa). Through its publications, StoryPeople Press strives to make the world a better place by spreading the words of laughter, imagination and inspiration. To see what other works are available, visit www.storypeoplepress.com.

StoryPeople features the the work of Brian Andreas and includes StoryPeople sculptures, colorful story prints, and books, all available in galleries and stores throughout the US, Canada and the EU (along with a few others scattered about the world), and on their web site. Please feel free to call or write for more information, or drop in on the web at www.storypeople.com

StoryPeople Press
113 E. Water St.
Decorah, IA 52101
USA

866.564.4552
563.382.8932
563.382.0263 FAX

StoryPeople
P.O. Box 7
Decorah, IA 52101
USA

800.476.7178
563.382.8060
563.382.0263 FAX